MW01230491

Dear Sheba...

Dear Sheba...

BILQEES MAUTHOOR

Text Karen Rust, on behalf of StoryTerrace

Design Nest Creative

Copyright © Bilqees Mauthoor

First print May 2021

CONTENTS

DEDICATION

I dedicate this book to my two wonderful sons,
Adam and Shak; the reasons why I live and breathe.
They are my strength and courage.

I become strong and brave because I wanted you both
to see the importance of a mother.
" Do good and serve
Your mother.
Then your Mother,
Then your Mother,
And then your father".
(Bukhari)

PROLOGUE

My Dear Reader,

My name is Sheba, you don't know me, but you soon will...

From being a child, the only daughter of her beloved father, my darling Belle was eager to find her perfect match, so she could fall in love and live happily ever after. But life did not turn out the way she expected. Affluent but naïve, little did she know her decisions about whom she loved would change her life in ways she never imagined. But even in her darkest moments, she believed there was more to life. Her special power was to know deep down that her destiny was written in pencil and she had the means to rewrite it in ink.

Born in the UK, Belle spent her secondary years on the remote island of Mauritius, tucked away in the Indian Ocean. This most beautiful birthplace of her ancestors lulled her into believing she wanted a simple life; to fall in love and marry, as was the norm there. But she wanted more. There was a fire inside her waiting to be ignited. Would it burst into flame or simply fade away?

I am the keeper of her diary, Belle's most trusted confidant. It contains the secrets of her deepest feelings, things she keeps locked away from all but me. Belle reveals her story throughout the book. But you will also get a chance to see entries of Belle's feelings from the most joyous and the darkest days of her life as she once wrote to me.

Belles' diary is a place where I can understand her, and maybe, my dear Reader, you can too...

CHAPTER ONE

"You have no idea what it is to have one's entire life reduced to a single moment."

— Daphne Bridgerton

During the sizzling summer of 1991 in Mauritius, the long-awaited wedding season had started. Women dressed in their finest clothing, each trying to outshine the other. I watched girls and women resplendent in skirts heavy with embroidery and delicate beading. Each gown I saw out-sparkled the next. The scent of fresh flowers and spicy food filled the warm air as mothers of young eligible bachelors scoured the wedding hall, seeking the perfect match.

There I was, just a few days shy of my 12th birthday. I had come of age and was no longer a little girl. I wondered what would become of me now I was a young lady. My gown showed off the changes in my body, my newly developed breasts sitting perfectly. Butterflies danced in my stomach as I realised I had all the curves in the right place.

I stood with my cousins at the edge of the room, scanning the fabled Rabitah wedding hall, which had hosted a thousand marriages. The promise of the day's festivities brought us to childish giggles. It took forever to get ready. I could never prepare enough because each wedding offered the chance for me to find my perfect match. Now, the wedding celebrations were underway. As soon as the bridegroom entered the room and met the bride with a kiss, we promenaded around the hall, meeting friends and family. Every girl longed to catch the right eye and make the match of the season.

'Belle. Come away from your cousins and sit with me.'

'Yes, mum,' I said, following my mother across the room with a quick backward glance.

'Do you need reminding that you are no longer a girl? You must act like a lady.'

"Yes mama, you don't need to remind me."

I sat at the table, sipping the drink my mother had placed in front of me. I studied the women closely and watched as a few men infiltrated the hall.

I was like an open book, emotions flitting across my face as I felt them, yet to learn the female art of concealment. The hours passed, whilst women gossiped, and the men discussed politics outside as though they were the prime minister himself. I would rather be with my cousins than sitting here, demure and bored. Across the room, I spied my mother talking to an auntie elegantly dressed in a royal blue gown. Her face was rosy, and her coiffured hair sat in light brown curls. I had never seen her before.

Mauritian life operated around a rigid social hierarchy, and my mother sat right at the top. Her pale complexion, beauty and breeding meant she could choose to speak only to those she deemed worthwhile. Yet, she was popular with all. I watched my mother negotiate the intricacies of this social setting, smiling politely as she ushered the unknown woman over. My mother had a natural way of socialising so eloquently, I simply couldn't fault her. I only hoped that one day I would become just like her. I longed to walk into a room of people and shine like the Mauritian sun.

'Belle, this is Saylia Aalam. We have been discussing her son, Isaac. He hopes to be a lawyer.'

A sudden flash of heat set my cheeks alight at the mention of her son. Could this Isaac be the one? Could he be my prince?

This conversation continued whilst Mrs Aalam examined me from head to toe with x-ray vision. Then, catching me off guard, she stood and cupped my face in her hands, her embrace wonderfully tender.

'Now young lady, you are to study hard, get a good education and, when you come of age, you will marry my son.'

It was done.

Was this the moment I'd prepared for all my life? All the years of aunties' advice on how to be a lady, and how to act in society brought to fruition? I should tell my cousins. No, I must not. I could not decide. I wanted to see my prince. Excusing myself, I wondered outdoors, giddy with the moment. The warm breeze lifted my dupatta scarf as I desperately searched for my father amongst the groups of men. No other man could talk to me without requesting an audience. I moved with the invisible wall of this protection cocooning me. I saw my father talking to the uncle who came with Mrs Aalam and there was a young man with them, his back towards me. From his frame, he looked a few years older, maybe in his senior years of college. I noted he was slim and smartly dressed in a suit with thick, luscious black locks. My father saw me approaching and broke off from the group, steering me away from the men to the shade of a palm tree. I had to think quickly of an excuse as to why I was outside without my mother.

'May I get you a drink, father?' I asked demurely, whilst trying to catch a glimpse of my potential prince.

My father tilted his head to one side, studying me, then nodded his approval of my offer. I dashed back into the hall and fetched a cool drink, straightening my skirt as I re-emerged. I was pleased to see my father waiting where I left him, hoping Isaac would still be out there too. My father took the drink whilst saying a few words to Isaac and Mr

Aalam. I was so caught up in the moment all I could do was stand and stare at Isaac. As I left with one arm folded into my father's arm, I couldn't resist another glance backwards. Isaac turned too, giving me a glimpse of an angular face with twinkling eyes that were dark as the night and intrinsically kind. A warm glow spread up my neck, and a smile played on my mouth, matching his. At that moment, as I whirled back into the hall, I was changed.

Dear Sheba,

You will never guess what happened today. I am betrothed! His name is Isaac and his family are good people. He is to become a lawyer, and I his wife when I finish my studies. His mother has made herself clear. I am to work hard. A lawyer cannot have an ill-educated wife. Oh, Sheba, I feel different, in a good way. I have become myself;

I have become Belle xx

My Dear Reader,

Here was Belle placing all her chances on the first man to call, hoping he'd give her a simple life and her happy ending. Was it just a puppy love?

Sometimes in life a young girl thinks she knows what she wants, when she doesn't even know what she doesn't yet know!

CHAPTER TWO

"I want every girl to know that her voice can change the world."

— Malala Yousafzai

Dear Sheba,

Our new home, Glenmore, is like a mansion! There is the most beautiful rose arch in the garden. It is like a secret garden with hidden gems, a perfect place for my wedding. I picture a marquee on the lawn; I hear music and laughter. There I am in a gown that makes every woman and girl wish they were me. And there he is, handsome, tall and dashing. He must be out there, Sheba. Maybe he is thinking of me?

Belle xx

My parents were hard-working people, my father a short but powerfully built, dark-skinned Mauritian and my mother a pale beauty, two things that were much prized in Mauritian culture. They met on a plane flying from Mauritius to England and fell in love. He had planned to travel on to France to join the navy, but everything changed after that plane journey. Settling in the Roman City outside of London, they trained as nurses and found jobs within the NHS in psychiatric institutions.

I joined my two older brothers, Noah and Yushra in June 1979, and the family was complete. I was the apple of my father's eye and he wrapped me in cotton wool and protected me from the world. Mum was beautiful and intelligent and always enjoyed reading books. Dad was a hands-on kind of man with ambitious plans to make his family comfortable.

We moved three times before we arrived at Glenmore and my parents kept each house, so by the time we got there, they owned four properties. Glenmore was an enormous, three-storey Victorian house. It stood at the top of a prominent hill and was striking with its white walls and double front door. In my child's mind there seemed to be endless bedrooms. I decided there were 22, which seems funny to me as an adult, because there were only actually nine! My brothers and I had the attic bedrooms, which were vast. During the great storm of 1987, the skyline window in the attic blew out in dramatic fashion. That house was made for drama and adventure.

The property's former owner, Mr Bryson, ran it as a B&B. My parents planned to do the same and eventually convert it into a nursing home. The house came fully furnished. It was like a wonderland to an eight-year-old with its velvet embossed wallpaper, dado rails and cornices, ornate fireplaces, bay windows and jungle of plants throughout.

In the living room, there was a dark mahogany sideboard inset with carved wooden roses. Inside we found a Royal Albert Old English Rose dinner service of 200 pieces. Apparently, the Brysons' entertained regularly and visitors from The House of Lords and Westminster were common. Mum only used the chinaware once when an important religious man came to the house. He was a Sufi and visited with the Sultan of Brunei. Mum hosted an extravagant dinner and I imagined the Sultan had a son whom I would marry in the garden and we'd have lots of children.

One of mine and my brother's favourite rooms in the house was the sun lounge. It was decorated with bright orange patterned wallpaper and filled with tropical house plants and over-stuffed sofas. It was a cheerful room and always warm. The younger of my brothers, Yushra, sometimes slept there and pretended he was camping in a jungle.

When we moved in, we discovered a secret door at the back of the stairs. It was easy to miss given it was papered in the same covering as the wall. It opened to reveal black stairs leading down to a chilly wine cellar. Down there, Dad discovered an old briefcase tied shut with a belt. It was like discovering ancient treasure. Inside, there were two oil paintings of the young Queen Elizabeth II and many Edward VII shillings.

The garden was magical. It was divided into several stepped sections, including a lawn, the dreamy rose arch, flower beds, a vegetable patch and a small, wooded area at the back. It was big enough for me to get lost in. Public tennis courts backed onto it and, in the summers, I recall the thwack of ball on racket, and the heady smell of lavender and rose wafting on the breeze. Mum held tea parties out there for the residents whenever the sun shone.

Along with the furniture, we inherited staff. The housekeeper was a podgy English lady named Josie, with an enormous nose and thick lips. She'd always ask us kids if we wanted an egg before school, making sure she fed us before she cooked for the guests. The gardener was tall and skinny with piercing blue eyes and white hair. There was a shed next to the kitchen only he used, which led to jokes about him keeping bodies in there. He terrified me.

We lived at Glenmore for four happy years. I got on well with my brothers, especially Yushra, who was only 18 months older than me. He and I were like chalk and cheese. He was an explorer and very mischievous. We had a bunch of cousins of similar ages and they'd come over at weekends. The Goonies movie came out and we were all obsessed with it. We got hold of some old maps and would run about the garden pretending we were aboard a pirate ship. Noah would be the pirate captain and I'd always be the princess who needed saving.

During this time, Mum and Dad were still working in nursing, taking opposite shifts so they could manage the B&B and the family. Then an awful thing happened. A troubled patient, a veteran from WWII, dragged my father from one side of a room to the other and broke his back. It left dad paralysed and unable to walk for months. This was not something my father took well. He was a proud man and a man who could handle himself, so this event bruised his ego. One day he announced that he'd had enough and was going back to Mauritius and taking us with him. I remember Yushra and I arriving home from school on a Friday and my older brother opening the door, telling us to hurry and get changed. We did as we were told, leaving our uniforms on our beds. Next thing a taxi was outside waiting and an aunty was there delivering food for us to eat on the ride to the airport. We were on the 10pm flight out of Heathrow and in Mauritius by the next day. That time we were there for a few months but didn't settle. We flew back on a Sunday flight and were home in time to go to school on the Monday. We put on the uniforms that still lay on our beds, replaced the rotten sandwiches in our school bags and set off as if those few months had never happened.

Dear Sheba,

I don't know if I am coming or going. I was suddenly in the heat of Mauritius, now I'm back in the damp and rain of England. I am so happy to be back at Glenmore, but my friends at school said I'm no longer part of their gang. Yushra prefers Mauritius, but I prefer the UK. I'm not sure what Noah thinks, but none of our thoughts matter, anyway. We are back here, and I don't know for how long. I'm glad I have you still.

Belle xx

My Dear Reader,

I felt for the girl. I know you will too. Back and forth she went several times between the two countries, never able to cultivate a best friend in either. Her education was disrupted, and much school was missed. BUT she was a pleasant girl and over time she became talented at meeting people of all ages and all types and putting them comfortably at ease. She did not know it then, but her experiences would teach her many more valuable lessons before she reached young womanhood...

CHAPTER THREE

"You may not control all the events that happen to you, but you can decide not to be reduced by them."

— Maya Angelou

Dear Sheba,

We are to move to Mauritius for good. I do not want to go, but what can I do? Dad has made his mind up and he will not listen. Does he not realise that I have a life here? I know Mum does not want to go either, but she stands by him as always. Will I have to do that someday, Sheba? Stand by my husband when I do not want to? At least you can come with me. You will be my only friend.

Belle xx

Mauritian life was a culture shock. We lived in a village called Quartier Militaire, referred to as Q. Militaire by the locals. Set on a high plateau in the centre of the island, it was wet and chilly there by Mauritian standards. The more modern house Dad was having built wasn't ready, so we moved into the eight-bedroomed house he'd inherited from his father. Built of a mixture of concrete, stone, wood and corrugated iron, with a red cement floor, it looked more makeshift than houses in the UK, but had survived since its days as a school in the 1800s. There was a latrine like a pit hole, which I found it very difficult to use. Every time I wanted to do a number two, I would have to go to my uncle's house across the road, which was so embarrassing. There was a stuffed stag's head on the wall that my grandfather shot. I used to tell my mum that I couldn't eat whilst looking at the thing. Some houses had three or four of them on the wall. They showed the prowess of the males in the house. One time my rich uncle took me, my dad and the boys hunting on his ranch by the beach. It was dark, but once my eyes adjusted, I saw hundreds of different coloured eyes looking at me from around the woods. The boys and the men jumped out with their guns, but I was too scared to go. Hunting was very much a norm for my uncles in those days, and my father loved it.

Even the basics differed from England. The water supply wasn't continuous and would only run for a couple of hours in the morning, maybe from six to eight, then for a couple more in the afternoon and again at night. The entire day revolved around the availability of water to manage the cooking, cleaning and bathing schedule. In the kitchen there were no modern conveniences like food mixers and microwaves. Our maid Lillian cooked food over a wood fire, which gave the rice a particular flavour. Outside there was a rock used for crushing spices with a pestle. There wasn't a refrigerator either, instead we stored food on newspaper lined shelves in a shady wooden cupboard with a chicken wire front. Lillian told me that on the day she was due to start school when she was nine, a friend told her not to go and to come to the sugarcane fields instead because you could earn money. Lillian's family were extremely poor, so she went to work instead of getting an education. She used to dance a Mauritian folk song called the Sega when she was working, using the top of a metal pot and a spoon to bang out the rhythm.

Mauritius was and still is renowned for its diversity with many families having Indian, Chinese and African heritage. My family originated from India, where my great-great-grandfather came from. In India there is a wide range of skin colour depending on the region you come from. It's true to say that fairer people get away with anything! My grandfather used to work for a white man in the Quarters who favoured him, so that's how he came to be successful. He had three wives and 15 children. Dad was his first-born son, so inherited a lot of his father's estate.

My grandfather owned a bakery and a petrol station and was the richest man in the district whilst he was alive. He died at 53, and that's when my dad inherited the house. My father followed suit and opened a bakery after we arrived in Q. Militaire. On the first couple of nights, Dad asked us to help make the bread as a family. He gave me the job of cutting thick slices of cooked bread and slathering them with butter and cheese to keep the rest of them going.

Village life was slow and stress free. The electricity supply was sporadic like the water supply. There were only two hours of TV programming each evening – the news, the weather and a sitcom. On a Thursday evening, there'd be an additional Indian movie. Sometimes the electricity cut out just when the TV came on. It ended at 9pm anyway, so it was candle lighting after that.

Q. Militaire was small and contained. A 10-minute walk away at the top of the road there was the bakery, the petrol station and the police station. Everyone else on the street was a relative, 50 or more cousins. It was a traditional place where most of the women kept house, cooked and sewed, whilst the men worked. Sewing was an important skill and everyone owned a Singer sewing machine, pronounced with a j rather than a g. Social occasions were a prominent part of the culture and dressing to impress was paramount, so girls learnt to sew from an early age. I watched my cousins but didn't try myself because my dad didn't want me to. Instead, I'd attend the Sunday Bazaar with a maid and pick a new fabric for my cousin, Masi, to make into a gown I'd seen on an Indian film. She was extremely skilled and made everything I asked for. I would mess about at my fittings, fidgeting and giggling, for which I received a cuff to the head. Girls used their skills in sewing and embroidery and crochet, to prepare their bridal trousseaus, making table linen, toilet covers, clothes and lingerie to store away for marriage. Between them, my cousins prepared mine and their own.

The locals spoke Creole, and I found the language a problem at first. I ran away from the Arabic classes and went to the Christian classes instead because they spoke English. I wasn't very academic and missed my school and friends from England. I confided in my maid, Lillian, who became like a second mother to me. She spoke Creole and before I knew it, I'd picked it up. Back in England, I'd enjoyed playing football and I tried to do the same in break times in Mauritius, only to be told that I couldn't because I was a girl. They told me I should walk around the field with other girls to get my exercise. I was having none of that and continued to play with the boys at break time, getting some other girls involved too. We ended up all getting letters home to our parents and had to stop, but I could feel myself railing against the system, even then.

I'd always dreamed of love and romance, of finding my perfect partner, but in Mauritius preparing girls for that was everything. My mind was full of romance, so it wasn't surprising that I fell for a boy I'd see at the school bus stop each day. Sometimes we'd sit together if my brothers weren't there. He couldn't speak to me which made our romance even more intense. We were in love for over a year and in all that time we barely spoke and never even touched hands.

Dear Sheba ,

When we moved to Mauritius, you were the only one who knew I didn't want to be here. The simplicity of life, the heat, a new language to master—it made my head spin, and I doubted I would cope. Yet here I am, a week away from my 12th birthday and I cannot imagine living anywhere else! Life is joyful here; Mum has settled and Dad has regained his happy self. At the weekend, we go to a wedding and I am excited about the gown Masi has made me. My body is changing, and I am proud to look in the mirror. I feel sparkly, Sheba. The future is beckoning.

Belle xx

My Dear Reader,

I was proud to watch Belle gaining priceless life experiences and adapting to new environments. She leant about the richness of culture and diversity and differences between the two cultures she sprang forth from. The local students competed highly to perform well at school, because education was valued more highly in Mauritius.

And I watched with a smile as a tiny spark inside of her ignited into a fire against injustice. She was told that she could not play football at school, that she must act like a girl. She poured her heart out to me about the unfairness of it all. She questioned who made such rules. An integral part of Belle roared into life that day…

CHAPTER FOUR

"When one door of happiness closes, another opens, but often we look so long at the closed door that we do not see the one that has opened for us."

— Helen Keller

Dear Sheba,

With all the other schools' boys asking me out all the time, I cannot help but think of Isaac. I think of him constantly. He is the most perfect thing to me. I see his eyes everywhere I look, so dark, so kind. I cannot wait to be his wife and to start our life together. Soon, I will be old enough for us to meet with chaperones. I can barely breathe when I think about that first meeting of being close to him. I know there will be electricity charging the air between us. I'm sure he feels the same way too.

Belle xx

Being betrothed gave me confidence. Every wedding celebration we attended, I aimed to look better than the last in case Isaac was there. We were back at the Rabitah Hall and I was almost 15 when I finally saw him again. It was a second cousin's wedding and the usual mix of embroidery and sparkle; spicy foods and adolescent body odour filled the boiling hot room. Standing with some cousins and an aunty, I caught sight of my elder brother, Noah, motioning to me from the doorway. I wandered over to him via the food table so as not to draw attention to my actions.

'He's here,' he hissed as soon as I reached him.

'Who?' I asked, my heart already missing a beat.

'You know who. Isaac.'

I gasped and stumbled forward. Noah caught me and rolled his eyes with a grin.

'Alright Cinderella, calm down.'

'Where is he?' I whispered, scanning the groups of men and older boys outside.

'Around the back of the hall in the shade.'

I couldn't hide my disappointment. 'I can see Dad just over there, nowhere near them. How am I going to see him?'

Noah shrugged. 'Sorry, sister. You know the rules.'

I returned to my cousins, my mind whirring as I tried to find a solution, but my body was two steps ahead of me. I awoke to faces peering at me from above.

'She's alright,' said my aunty, helping me to sit up. 'You gave us a fright, young lady.'

My mum appeared, the room parting to let her through as normal.

'Let's get her some fresh air,' she said, taking my arm and leading me outside.

She sat me in a chair under a palm tree and studied my face. 'You look pale. I shall get you a cold drink,' she said and disappeared back into the hall. I sat up straight, smoothing my hair and straightening my dress. The men carried on with their political discussion as if I wasn't there. I fixed my eyes onto the corner of the hall. Please come to me, I implored the universe. And he did. Time slowed as he appeared around the corner with his father, deep in conversation, chin down. He wore another smart suit, tailored perfectly to show off his narrow waist and widening shoulders. His black hair had grown longer, falling across his eyes. He swept the hair back with his hand and in that moment, he looked up and our eyes met. Every nerve in my skin tingled. His smile warmed my soul, and I hope mine did the same for him.

'Belle?' said my mother with impatience in her voice. I looked at her as she turned to see where I'd been looking. 'I see,' she said and stood directly in front of me, blocking my view. 'Drink this and let's get you back inside.'

'When can I have a chaperoned meeting?' I asked, throwing caution to the wind.

'Not long, Belle. Be patient,' she said with a smile as she helped me up, linked her arm through mine and steered me back into the hall.

I felt restless after that encounter. It seemed stupid for us not to meet now. Maybe Mum sensed that because only a few weeks after my 15th birthday, the Aalam's came to visit. It was a gathering to which I wasn't invited, so I paced my bedroom with sweaty palms, wondering what was being said.

'Quick!' shouted Lillian, rushing me out onto the veranda so I could see them as they left. They were walking towards their car, Isaac with his back to me again. Was I only ever to see him from behind? Lillian suddenly let out a whistle. I looked at her in shock as she ducked down below the veranda railing. Mr and Mrs Aalam were already in the car, but Isaac turned and looked up. My breath caught in my ribcage as I tried to assess the situation. I was going to kill Lillian. His face broke into a grin and he raised his fingers in a stationary wave just enough for me to see, but not his parents. I raised mine back, and he was gone.

That grin kept me going for months, but then something unexpected happened. A Mauritian family visiting from England came to dinner. After the guests had gone, my parents called me downstairs and told me that the visitors had issued a proposal on behalf of their son and they had accepted. I looked at them, dumfounded. But I was to marry Isaac. Wasn't I? Mum saw my expression and pulled me to sit beside her, stroking my arm as Dad spoke.

'It is okay, Belle. This may seem confusing, but we have made this decision for the best. Our guests tonight are a well-respected family, and their son is a qualified lawyer. He is their only son, so your relationship will be their focus. We will move back to England in 18 months so you can marry and live there.' I nodded and hugged my parents, but once in bed, I sobbed myself to sleep.

Dear Sheba,

A bomb has exploded in my life today. The future I had planned with Isaac, the house, the children, the travel and adventures we would have, is all gone up. I know my parents have my best interests at heart, but this pain is too much for me to bear.
Belle xx

My parents understood the etiquette and invited Mr and Mrs Aalam to explain the situation. Before they left, Mrs Aalam asked to see me. She held my face as she had before and wished me well. Then she gave me a pair of gold earrings.

'I brought them for my daughter-in-law to be, but now they will be for the daughter-in-law I missed.'

I could not stop a tear from rolling down my cheek at her words. My time in Mauritius had been precious with all its culture and rich diversity. I had been sure of my future with Isaac, but now all was uncertain.

My Dear Reader

It broke my heart to see Belle so upset, but all I could do was soak up her words and her tears on these pages. Belle was a good girl, always calm and sensible. She would never displease her parents, for she knew their intentions were good. I hoped the return to our homeland would bring a silver lining to her cloud of sadness, but nothing could prepare us for what was to come...

CHAPTER FIVE

"Do not tame the wolf inside you just because you've met someone who doesn't have the courage to handle you."

— Belle Estreller

Dear Sheba ,

I am back in England and feel as out of sorts as when I first arrived in Mauritius. Everything seems odd, from the temperature to the smells and sounds. I am to meet Rayhan later, but I'm told he likes to be called Ray. I am scared I will feel like a child beside him. Isaac was five years older than me, but Ray is seven. On top of the age difference, Ray has grown up in England and is more, how would you say, worldly. I trust my parents' choice, of course I do, but I have a strange feeling about Ray.

Belle xx

was 18 and in the second year of sixth form. It was almost a year since we'd returned from Mauritius and I met Ray for that first time. It hadn't taken long for me to fall for him. He was charming, handsome and a little cocky. We met every couple of weeks with a family member as a chaperone. What they didn't know was that we met in between without. Someone would come with a message that Ray was outside the sixth form block in his beloved Mercedes and I would run to meet him and fall into his arms. Sometimes he'd turn up when he knew Dad wasn't getting me, usually when I had a football match after school. He'd watch some of the game and then drop me around the corner from home. Other times, he'd engineer my pickup from school by visiting mum and dad with his mother for tea in the afternoon. Then he'd suggest that the adults could keep talking and he would come and get me. He'd pick me up and drive somewhere quiet so we could kiss in the car before he drove me home. On Valentine's day he turned up at sixth form with a teddy, chocolates, flowers and a card. I couldn't take them home because we weren't supposed to meet, so friends had to smuggle them to me at home bit by bit. I can understand why people find affairs so exciting, because the illicit nature of our meetings heightened the longing.

Isaac crossed my mind occasionally, but we never even spoke, whereas what I had with Ray was real. The more I saw him, the less I thought of Isaac. As the wedding approached, so did my A-level exams. Tensions built and Ray became harder to read. My parents gave us permission to shop for wedding rings together in Southall. I told him I didn't like gold, so would prefer a white gold ring. He became furious about the waste of money I was proposing, said the wedding was costing a fortune and he had a budget in mind. We had a row in the shop and I ended up picking a gold band to pacify him. I tried to explain it away as pre-wedding jitters, but my gut was not so sure. Then I went for a professional photoshoot. My parents paid for it and I was excited to be doing something so grown up. I asked Ray to pick me up from the session, intending to ask him to select a photograph as my wedding gift to him. I envisaged an intimate moment, holding hands in the dark as we viewed the photographs on the big screen, him enchanted by what he saw. Instead, he became angry and talked about my wasting money again. The photographer asked me if I was alright because of Ray's aggressive demeanour. He dropped me home, and I went to my room and cried. He wasn't even the one paying for it, it was my gift to give. I decided he wouldn't have any of the photos, I would keep the one I'd chosen for myself.

I noticed that he often got upset after a phone call. One time I asked him what was wrong when we were in the car and he told me never to ask questions like that again. A couple of minutes later, when we pulled up at traffic lights near to Waterlow park, he told me to 'fuck off and get out of my car'. I was stunned. I got out, and he drove off. I ran into the park and found a bench in a secluded area. I sat there crying for ages, not noticing how wet I was getting from the rain. I felt numb and couldn't understand what was going on with this man I loved. A woman in jogging clothes appeared next to me and asked if I was okay. We chatted, and it seemed as if she knew my pain.

'Do I get married or not?' I wondered, as much to myself as to her.

'I think it's a mistake,' she said. 'You haven't lived your life yet and you don't know what you want.'

I frowned at the thought of not getting married. 'But I have to. My parents have spent so much money on it and guests are arriving soon.'

She looked at me sombrely. 'Well, you'll have to face the consequences then.'

I looked away, and when I looked back, she was gone. My mind tried to make sense of our conversation. Had it even happened? I stumbled out of the park as the sun was setting and found Ray standing there. He rushed over to me, all apologies, and draped his jacket around my shoulders. He said he was stressed and made excuses for his behaviour, but I was too numb with shock to forgive him.

My A-level exams were only weeks away, and wedding plans were on my parents' minds every day. Because I was their only daughter, they were throwing an enormous party, with over 750 guests invited. In Mauritian culture, it is commonplace to bring any house guests you have in other words, gate crashing was extremely common.

Dear Sheba,

That person, yes him I loved and trusted, is a b******.
He didn't go to Cyprus on his stag do, instead he went to
Ibiza – party central! He lied to me. I only know because
there was a train strike, so I went with a friend to pick
them up as a surprise. At the terminal, it was clear there
was no flight landing from Cyprus, only Ibiza, but still
he got angry and lied to my face. Back at his place, he was
unpacking clothes, and a receipt fell out of his trousers.
I picked it up. It was from a car hire company. In Ibiza.
Help me, Sheba. What am I to do? The wedding is
too close to cancel. I am to marry a beast. He has
lost my trust and I do not know him anymore. I
know I am marrying the wrong man. Sheba,
keep me strong.

Belle xxx

The wedding was an event that people talked about for
years. It was July, and the weather was perfect. My wedding
dress was stunning, pure white with a 5m train embroidered
with roses. The celebration took place over three days and
across two halls decorated in gold. There was a sit down
three course meal and a disco for the 1,350 guests who
attended. When we cut the wedding cake, indoor fireworks
filled the room with light.

Lovely as it all looked, I knew it was a mistake. Noah
and Yushra were in the Bentley with me as I headed to
the ceremony. The driver reached a junction where going

straight on took us to the airport and turning right to the wedding. He turned and looked at me, told me about the choice and asked which way I'd like to go. Maybe it was a joke he made every time he got to that junction, but it felt like he was talking to my soul.

'Straight to the airport,' I said without hesitation, just as Noah told him to turn right. We turned right, and I had the perfect fairytale wedding with only one detail wrong. My Mr Darcy was absent. For the first time in a while, my thoughts strayed back to Isaac.

My Dear Reader,

Like me, I am sure you are watching our Belle with a pain in your heart. She had the fairytale wedding, the event of the year, the grand decorations and beautiful gown, but under the facade of perfection, she was uneasy. And who could blame her! She had no choice to marry once she was so far into the process, otherwise, she'd be seen as tarnished goods. She wanted desperately to believe it was nerves causing Ray, to act as he was. I wanted to believe it too, for her.

How about you?

CHAPTER SIX

You cannot develop character in ease and quiet. Only through experience of trial and suffering can the soul be strengthened, ambition inspired, and success achieved.

— Helen Keller

Dear Sheba,

I haven't spoken to you for a while because it takes all of my energy just to do the basics in life each day. I have been married for six long months and am studying nursing at University. One brings me immense pleasure, one does not. I'm sure you can guess. Ray is a difficult man with a terrible temper. Two weeks after the wedding, he threw our wedding presents at me. I was bruised and terrified to see the fate I feared for myself become reality. I cannot please him. I try to cook and clean, but it is not good enough. He has thrown hot pans and plates of food at me. I never know what mood he will be in and pray for good ones. I am broken, Sheba.

Belle xx

At university, I was a strong, confident woman, the one who made her friends laugh. My friends there thought it was ridiculous that I married so young, but they were accepting of it. Ray let me have a night out with them and stay over at their uni residences once a fortnight. We'd have the most fabulous time, and I'd feel like a normal 19-year-old for a few hours, but then I'd get up early and go home to make breakfast for him. I'm sure they realised I was unhappy, but they left it for me to come to them and I wasn't ready to admit my feelings to anyone.

Ray's moods seemed to come and go in cycles. For a while, things would be almost normal and I'd wonder if I was overplaying the situation in my mind. But then he'd lose his temper about something or belittle me in front of friends or family, and I'd be walking around on eggshells again.

Then Ray's father died. I was in Mauritius when it happened and missed the funeral. When I came back, his mother was living with us. I felt like an outsider but having her there stopped the physical violence. After six months she returned to her flat and the mental and physical abuse escalated again. Every day was a series of choices and decisions aimed at keeping the peace. I knew the marriage needed to end, but I wasn't strong enough to do it. Occasionally I tried to be a dutiful daughter and wife and make things work. After one such night where we'd had a takeaway together and I'd done the whole candles and bedroom thing, we had another row and he left for his mother's. He spent Ramadan there, and the relief was palpable. I hoped he'd never come back.

Then I discovered I was pregnant. A wondrous discovery spoiled by the knowledge that my escape route had just closed.

My Dear Reader,

Restock the tissues, the popcorn and the soda, especially the tissues my dear soul, because this ride is going to get bumpy...

CHAPTER SEVEN

"Think like a queen. A queen is not afraid to fail. Failure is another steppingstone to greatness,"

— Oprah Winfrey

Dear Sheba,

What am I to do? I am carrying his child. I want the child, but I do not want him. I am in a terrible mess.

Belle xx

asked to meet Ray on the night before EID at Alexandra Palace. I told him I was pregnant and he surprised me by being delighted. I said I wasn't sure this was the right time for us, but he would hear none of that.

Pregnancy made him kinder and my parents moved

closer, so life was more peaceful for a while. I was in the third year of my course when I discovered I was pregnant and considered dropping out, heavily encouraged by Ray. My course tutor was fierce about me staying and told me that nursing was something I would always have, so to keep at it. Maybe she suspected something was wrong? I don't know, but I am eternally grateful to her for pushing me to continue.

Nursing was my escape. Belle the nurse was happy, outgoing, a joker. My time on the wards flew by as I lost myself in the trusted process of assessing each patient, identifying the problem, planning treatment for each symptom, then evaluating and revising to get the best results. The woman I became at work was the opposite of the meek, apologetic woman I was at home. I was living a double life and there were two very different Belle's inhabiting the world.

Then the baby came and I fell in love with Adam the moment I saw his face. He was a calm baby which was lucky because Ray hated the sound of him crying and would become enraged on the odd occasion he was difficult to soothe. My parents had Adam when I was on shifts and studying, they brought him up for most of his first year. I couldn't have managed without them.

Ray was never violent to Adam, but it didn't take long for his violence to return with me. Our marriage stumbled along. I knew I should leave but, with the baby to care for and nursing using up my energy, I had nothing left to get myself out with.

It was a proud day when I completed my degree, specialising in paediatrics. I started working straight away on the paediatric ward where I'd had a placement. My colleagues became like a second family and although I didn't tell them much of what went on at home, I'm sure they had some idea.

It's funny how you learn to cope with a situation. How something that once seemed unthinkable can become normal. At work, I grew as a person and at home I shrunk.

Then one day, I was rushing to collect Adam from Mum's after my shift. The traffic had been dreadful, and I had felt ill all day. As I pulled up, I noticed a car I didn't recognise on their driveway. A smart-looking Audi. Visitors were common in our culture, so I didn't think too much about it. The front door was unlocked, as usual, and I called out 'hello' as I entered the hallway. I froze where I stood. There in front of me, walking down the hallway, was Isaac. It felt like a dream. I looked into those dark, kind eyes and felt a load lift from my shoulders.

'Good evening, Belle,' he said smiling.

'Good evening, Isaac,' I replied, unable to think of anything else to say.

A breathless moment hung in the air between us, and then he moved down the hallway towards me. Part of me longed for him to pull me into an embrace, but that was a long-gone dream. I was a married woman. Most likely he was a married man. I moved to the side, so he could pass me, and as he did so the back of his hand brushed mine so lightly, I wondered if I'd imagined it. I took a deep breath and turned, but the front door was already closing behind him. I steadied myself against the wall, waiting for my heart to slow a little before I called out 'hello' again.

After that moment in the hall, two things happened; I found out I was pregnant again and I knew I would leave Ray. It was as if the sight of Isaac had reignited something in me, and I felt the old Belle come back to life. She had been missing for a long time.

I needed to choose my moment and knew it couldn't be whilst I was pregnant. He'd never hit me whilst I was pregnant with Adam, but I didn't want to chance it. Twelve months after Shak was born, I told Ray that I didn't love him. It was a phrase that had been wedged in my chest like a splinter for so long, and now I'd finally said it. Ray was furious. He didn't care if I loved him or not; I wasn't leaving. I argued back for once and he attacked me with his electric razor, which was lying in the bedroom. He stabbed me repeatedly in the head with it whilst Shak was in my arms. I ran downstairs with my head throbbing and my hair pulled out of its ponytail and put Shak in the living room. There were French doors through to the conservatory and I ran in there to get some baby food and nappies to take with me. As I bent down to grab the things, Ray was suddenly there, and he pushed me hard, so I sprawled out onto the floor. Then he kicked me, punched me and pulled my hair whilst calling me names. I could see Shak with his hands against the glass of the French doors, screaming. My body was there, but it felt like my soul had left. Shak was crying so much he choked. I screamed at Ray to let me go to the baby and in the middle of the shouting his mobile rang in the bedroom. He ran upstairs to get it and I grabbed Shak and the car keys and ran away.

I stayed at my mums for the rest of the day. I could not tell my parents anything, I made excuses all the time that I was sick and exhausted. Ray came around and begged me to go back, asking me what kind of mother would separate her boys from their father. The attack had weakened my resolve and I went home with him. Over the next couple of weeks, he worked hard on me repeating the mother slur and reminding me I'd be homeless if we separated because I wouldn't be able to afford the house on my own and he would give me nothing. He said that he knew law so well that if I tried to divorce him, he'd get everything, including the boys.

Dear Sheba,

I want my life to end and this pain to stop, but I must keep going for my boys. He slaps me, punches me, derides me. I do not want these things.

> I want to be a woman in a suit
> I want to be a wonderful mother to my boys
> I want to love a man and be happy
> I want my freedom
> I want to help those in need.

But no-one listens. Maybe my life is to always be a punchbag, a floorboard for him to stamp on. I am not thinking straight Sheba; I am scared.

Belle xx

My Dear Reader,

That list brought a tear to my eye. Do you have one of those tissues spare? There was the Belle I saw back in Mauritius, the girl who'd argue her right to kick a ball. She wanted to wear a suit and shuck off the oversized t-shirts and jeans that had become her uniform. She wanted to style her hair instead of scrape it back into a ponytail. Every swear word, every beating had dampened that flame but, in that list, I saw a flicker and that is all a fire needs...

At work, it felt like the universe was sending me messages. Every other mother whose child I cared for in the ward showed signs of domestic abuse. I realised it wasn't just me and friends told me that what I was experiencing wasn't a normal part of marriage; it was abuse. Aptly, it was 1st April 2006, when the seminal moment came. The boys were with my cousin and I was in my uniform ready to start a shift when a row escalated. Ray attacked me again. I was frightened for my life, but I got away from him long enough to call work. I was beyond exhausted with my life and simply said.

'I can't come to work today; my husband is beating me.'

Work called the Police who arrived quickly and arrested Ray. They took him away for a night in the cells. One officer looked at my uniform and said, 'You're a nurse, you're one of us, I'm not going to let this go.'

It was the final straw. I didn't want my boys to grow up in an environment like this; I wanted them to see me strong. I made the decision that he was out of my life for good. I took a chance on life. I knew I deserved better and somewhere out there lay the future where I would find peace and old wounds would heal.

After the police left, I took off my shoes and threw them in the air, so they landed higgledy-piggledy in the middle of the room. Ray would never have allowed such a thing. I left them where they landed. A symbol of the new Belle.

CHAPTER EIGHT

"The question isn't who is going to let me, it's who is going to stop me."

— Ayn Rand

Dear Sheba,

I am free, so why do I feel so bad? A single mother with two young children. This is not what I dreamed of all those years ago. Ray refuses to pay the mortgage or help me financially. He is the one who caused this, yet he can remarry and carries no shame whereas I, the victim, am seen as tarnished goods. What chance do I have of love now? Real love? Love that doesn't hurt. I will raise my boys to know that women are strong and equal to them. I will raise them to respect women and make good husbands.

Belle xx

took some time off work to get my head together. It was like a form of PTSD. I struggled to come to terms with what had happened, to understand how I had let it happen. And what to do now? It was a dark time. Ray refused to pay the mortgage and the mortgage company was ready to repossess. On the advice of a friend, I took myself to the council with a bin bag full of clothes and told them I was being made homeless. She said to take the boys too, but I couldn't bring myself to do that and left them with my cousin. As I sat opposite the lady behind the counter, I imagined how I must appear to her in my jeans, black jumper, and no make-up, grasping a bin bag. It was a bleak moment. When I got home, my brother Yushra called from Mauritius. He'd had a nightmare with me in it and wanted to hear my voice. 'Are you alright, sister?' he asked. I hadn't told my family in Mauritius anything, so it was quite a shock for him. He was my saviour. He helped me and my family by supporting me through the breakup and settled all matters for me so I could live a decent life.

As I recovered, I had to admit that nursing, the thing that had kept me sane for the last 10 years, was not compatible with my new single mother status. I had no choice but to look for a job with regular daytime hours that worked around my boys' schedules.

After interviews, I was repeatedly told I'd performed well, but there were other more qualified people who had got the job. It was soul destroying. It was coming up to

Adam's birthday, and I was short of money, so I sold some of my gold to pay for his party and to make ends meet. I was a complete mess and too scared to tell anyone. I think that may have been my lowest point. I had no job or self-confidence, and life could not get any worse. Then the strangest thing happened to me. I saw an article in a magazine about trying something different and it sparked my imagination. Before I knew it, I was auditioning for a part in a community play at the local theatre. It took audacity for me to attend. It was so unlike anything I'd done before. The thrill of being told I had a part in was such a high. Being part of a cast and crew of 60 people and the buzz of the applause during the show was the best morale boost I could have asked for.

Then, I heard from a nursing recruitment agency about an interview. The job sounded perfect. I'd be managing nurses as a clinical lead, finding them placements, and looking after their day-to-day needs. It was a normal 9-5 office job, but I could use my years of nursing experience. I couldn't have wanted a job more.

The interview was in Woodford Green, but, because I was so nervous, I headed to Wood Green. I was late and lost and, in a panic. When they called to see where I was, I realised my mistake and was gutted. They must have heard that in my voice because they told me to take a deep breath, reroute myself, and they'd do the interview at the end of the day. The CEO came into the room and asked me what I wanted out of the role.

'To wear a suit, have the reddest lips and painted nails,' I said. I'd had enough of the jeans and t-shirts. It was time for the change I'd promised myself.

He liked that, and I got the job. I think he may have guessed that my personal life was troubled. The job allowed my people skills to come to the fore, and my confidence grew. The jigsaw of my life was slowly coming together. Now I had a house, my boys, friends and a job that suited me. There was just one piece missing.

Dear Sheba,

I feel the dark clouds parting after living in their shadow for so long. For the first time in an age, I feel hopeful. Hopeful of what lies ahead of me. If life is a journey, mine has been rocky, and I have spent years at the bottom of the abyss. I have asked; Why me? Why me? Now I know it is because God made me that way to experience that situation and understand it. I must use my experience to help others.

Belle xx

Late one night I flicked through Facebook. I'd been thinking about it for weeks, but I was scared to look. Should I? I tapped the search function and typed in Isaac Aalam, my heart quickening even before I hit return. There was only one, and it was him. With clammy hands, I clicked onto his profile. His profile picture showed him with two girls, maybe a couple of years younger than my boys. There was no sign of a wife in any of his profile pictures, just the girls and a black Labrador. What did that mean? Well Belle, I asked myself, are you going to click or not? My finger hovered over the friend request button. I shouldn't, but then again… After all I'd been through, why not? I clicked the button and dropped my phone onto the sofa like a hot brick.

My Dear Reader,

Things are on the up. After a decade of despair, Belle is hopeful again, and it fills me with joy. She is rediscovering herself. Even though it was humiliating sitting at the council customer service desk she saw a big brown door marked "For Staff Only". Little did she know that those very same doors would, one day, be open to her.

The blossoms are finally blooming for her. The missing piece of her jigsaw of life, namely love, is the hardest to find, as many of you will know from hard experience. How many frogs will she have to kiss?

Let us find out…

CHAPTER NINE

"Women belong in all places where decisions are being made… It shouldn't be that women are the exception."

— Ruth Bader Ginsburg

Dear Sheba ,

What have I done, sending Isaac a friend request? I must have lost my mind. I have cancelled the request. I'm sure he didn't see it as it was silly o'clock when I sent it and even sillier o'clock when I cancelled it. Love hasn't worked out for me, and maybe there is a reason. Life is good again, and I mustn't spoil it. I have achieved more than I ever thought I was capable of, and there is more to come. Being an entrepreneur, Sheba, that is my ultimate aim. To own a business that helps people and maybe a house by the sea. My boys will fly the nest one day, but I am at peace with that. I am raising them well.

Belle xx

t's funny how unexpected moments in life can propel you onto an alternative course. One night, there was a knock at the door and I reluctantly opened it to find a labour activist there. I chatted with him politely, thinking of ways to end the conversation, but became passionate as we talked. He said I should attend a local council meeting and took my number. I didn't think too much about it until a lady named Anne called and asked if I'd like to go to the meeting with her. I didn't know at that point that she'd become my mentor and an important figure in my life.

Before I knew it, I was being encouraged to stand as a councillor.

'I don't even know how to spell it!' I said.

But I was hooked. I'd spent my childhood listening to the men talk about politics, you'd swear my uncle was the prime minister the way he went on, but none of them got anything done. I was duly elected and made it my mission to bring change. Having the letters Cllr after my name gave me a mandate to do just that. I threw myself into council work over the next couple of years and became the Women's Officer for the town's Labour party.

Women's issues and inclusivity were a focus for me, and when the lockdown kicked in, it became clear that those issues would only be exacerbated by the pandemic. Over the years, I've been lucky to meet many inspirational women including Harriet Harman, Stella Creasy and the former first female president of Mauritius. I hoped to meet

Jess Philips, Lisa Nandy and Angela Rayner for a coffee in parliament one day - imagine that conversation!

Although I was not the brightest at school, having applied for elite schools I never got accepted. But another opportunity came my way. I was selected from more than a 1000 applicants to attend a five-day residential leadership course at a very prestigious university to run through one of the most inspiring pathway to success programmes. Education, education education, well, yes, it does do the trick! The course made me realise my true potential and nothing is going to stop me now.

Throughout it all, Anne was my rock, a true feminist who gave me my voice. And I wanted to pass that gift on to women everywhere with an absolute passion.

I wanted our girls to grow up in a safe space and not miss out on opportunities for the best education; an education that could make them shine like the brightest star. I wanted young girls to grow up feeling strong and ambitious and standing for what they believe in. I wanted all married women and women in a relationship to know they deserved to feel loved and valued. I wanted working mums to be enabled, so their hard work paid off and brought a better life for their families. I wanted to see more women taking on leadership roles and mentoring younger women and girls, so they knew they could reach for the stars too. I wanted to ensure women had access to the right medical services at the right time and to make sure men were educated about the physical changes women went through in life, so they were best prepared to support their partner. I wanted women and girls to be safe when they walked down a street, with no fear of harassment or assault. Most of all, I wanted to end all violence against women and girls.

Maybe my interest in politics had always been there, but from the moment I was told I could not play football at school, it had flickered into life. I had always cared about people and nursing had given me an outlet for that. Now I had politics, and when I was elected Chairman for the Council, I knew I had a mandate: to convert the pain I had suffered into true purpose, and I would.

One day, I entered a zoom meeting with various local figures from business and politics, to discuss a new initiative on ending violence against women. Another name flashed up in the waiting room and my heart missed a beat. Isaac Aalam. What? I must have misread. I clicked for them to enter. Someone was talking to me, but I wasn't hearing a word they said as I waited for the video to pop up. It was him! A flush crept up my face, and I knew I must be bright red. I cleared my throat.

'Welcome all and thank you for coming today and showing your interest in this initiative…'

I could barely breathe, let alone talk. Somehow, I got through the meeting. Isaac did not show that we knew each other. He was the perfect gentlemen. From what he said, it was obvious he was aware of much of my work with charities and women in the area. My heart swelled to know that. It was the oddest meeting I have ever been in. Anne stepped in twice and kept things going when I was lost for words. I knew she'd be ringing me afterwards to see why my usual efficient self was absent from that meeting!

Afterwards, I felt so many emotions as I fixed myself a cup of tea. He still made me breathless and morphed me back into the 12-year-old I'd been when I met him, with a head full of romance and love. As expected, Anne called and grilled me on my odd behaviour. In her usual firm but encouraging style, she told me to get in contact with Isaac and arrange a socially distanced coffee. She said I could use the pretence of the initiative for the meeting and then figure out if he was interested. I was mortified. There was no way I could do such a thing. I told her to drop it, but it was on my mind every day.

The list of things I'd told Sheba I wanted in life many moons ago was almost complete. Love was the missing item, but I figured I could still enjoy other people's romance when I received an invitation to my cousin's daughter's wedding. It was the next generation down that was getting married now, and that made me feel old.

My preparation for the wedding was much shorter than when I was younger. I looked at myself in the mirror before I left. Adam came in behind me, a young man himself now, and told me I looked beautiful. I grinned. 'I scrub up okay,' I said, and he kissed me on the cheek.

The wedding was smaller than normal because of restrictions, but there were still plenty of cousins and friends, many of whom I hadn't seen since the divorce. Enough time had passed now for that to no longer be an issue, and it was a lovely day of catching up with people. The boys were chatting to some of their cousins and I was people watching, checking out outfits and thinking about the extravagant gowns we wore in Mauritius. Like a figure stepping into that daydream, there was Isaac across the room. I gasped, my face flushing at the sight of him. He caught my eye, smiled and walked across the dance floor. I took a sip of my drink to wet my dry mouth.

'Belle, how are you?' he said, sitting in the empty chair next to me. It felt odd to speak one on one, but of course, we were no longer teenagers and we could do that now. Still, the inner-teen Belle was tongue tied and ready to run. I steeled myself and spoke normally. An hour passed, and we were still chatting. We talked about the new initiative and Anne was right, that was a good starting point. He said he'd seen an article about me in the local newspaper, and that's how he'd heard about my work. We chatted about our favourite charities, politics, his pro-bono work as a lawyer and my work with nurses. The one subject we danced around was our relationship status. He didn't say he knew mine, and it hadn't been in the article, so maybe he didn't. Finally, he told me he was a widower. His wife had died three years ago in a car crash. I felt awful for his loss, but a bit of me was pleased he was single. That thought disgusted me. He looked at me, expecting me to reciprocate on the relationship status front. I stammered out that I had two boys and was married. I couldn't bring myself to tell him I wasn't. The shame of the divorce and the feeling I'd just had made me feel unworthy. He fixed me with a stare so intense it turned my insides to jelly.

'I thought we might take a chance,' he said.

I stood, toppling my chair over backwards. 'I can't, I'm sorry. My vows are sacred to me.' I grabbed my bag, gathered the boys and left.

Next morning, I sipped my coffee and caught up on the news on my phone. A ping made me swipe upwards. There was a friend request on Facebook. From Isaac.

My Dear Reader,

In life you should listen and accept what Mother Nature tells you. Belle might be blossoming in the political arena, but in the arena of love? There she was still hurting, and the ice-queen within had erected a solid barrier around her heart. Understandable of course. We've all been there to some extent, have we not? Mother Nature was sending the sun in the form of Isaac Aalam and eventually Belle would have to decide whether to let that sunlight into her heart...

CHAPTER TEN

"On the left side of a strong woman, stands a strong man; he is strengthened by her character."

— Ellen J. Barrier

Dear Sheba,

I faced the situation last night and told Isaac that I am divorced. Turns out that he knew, but after I said I wasn't, he didn't want to embarrass me and has been waiting all this time for me to fess up. I was mortified, but he laughed, told me not to worry. Said he understood. All the feelings I had for him as a teenager are back, only better because they are reflected through the mirror of wisdom my experience has given me. Am I being silly to imagine my fairy-tale wedding again, but this time with my real Mr Darcy in attendance? Please say no, Sheba. I want it to be possible.

Belle xx

saac was in my life. I could say that truthfully. We were digital friends mostly, commenting on each other's posts and sharing private messages about growing up in Mauritius. I called him to tell him about my lie, and then we had a lengthy conversation. After that we spoke regularly. His political views were in sync with mine, and his parents had brought him up to help those in need. I felt I could tell him anything. He even liked football and historic dramas and we joked about going to a match or the cinema together when things got back to normal.

Recently, I'd had some harrowing calls with some of my nurses working on the covid wards. The vast numbers of patients, the PPE, the staff shortages and the deaths, were taking a toll on many. An experienced nurse called me at the end of her shift in tears. That day they were so short on ITU beds, she'd had to turn basement operating theatres into extra ITU's and try to train nurses who'd never worked in that field before on the spot. She was exhausted and traumatised, and it took an hour to talk through things with her. She was going through the menopause, so wearing the full PPE gear made her sweat so much it left her gasping for water. It made me realise how much nurses neglect their own bodies to saves lives. Her experiences chilled me and made me even more determined to make a difference through politics.

Isaac was the perfect person to talk things like that through with. He made me feel utterly safe and accepted.

The polar opposite of my ex-husband. A few weeks later, whilst we were chatting, he mentioned he'd be away for a couple of weeks, visiting his house in Cornwall. It'd been locked up for a lot of the year, so he needed to check everything was okay down there. I said I'd look forward to seeing the photos on Facebook and told him to give Ross Poldark a kiss from me, which made him laugh.

After I hung up, I realised I was jealous, jealous of him going to Cornwall without me. I was a huge fan of the Poldark TV series, and he knew that. I'd promised myself I would visit the area one day. The more I thought about him being down there, the more agitated I felt and out of nowhere a notion popped into my head. I would go down there myself. Not to see Isaac, of course, but to experience the place I'd watched on TV for so long.

Within an hour, I'd booked a long weekend off work and found myself a boutique hotel close to Holywell Bay, where they filmed many of the beach scenes in Poldark. The boys were old enough to look after themselves, so it was just me going. The idea thrilled and terrified me in equal measure. I'd never taken a holiday on my own.

Cornwall was an absolute dream. On every cliff and beach, I fully expected to see Ross Poldark running towards me with his dark hair blowing in the wind. Being on my own was empowering, and I promised to give myself a trip like this every year. The boutique hotel was gorgeous, the food and mocktails were excellent and the fresh air a tonic. My room was named the butterfly suite, with beautiful butterfly wallpaper and a to-die-for view of the valley. The hotel was run by a lovely lady named Karen and her daughters, and she and I had an instant connection. She accompanied me on Poldark tours, and we spent hours discovering the similarities of our experiences in life. It was a comfort to know that it wasn't just me that had endured difficulties.

Walking through the wilds of that place, I felt a new future come into focus. I could imagine myself living here and running a business I'd always wanted to set up. Politics was portable and my boys were off to University soon. A new dawn was on the horizon.

The sunset over the beach on my last night was so beautiful I couldn't resist a selfie against it. I posted and tagged it on Facebook and the boys commented on it, saying how amazing Cornwall looked and maybe they should have come.

The next morning, I set off early for my last walk across Holywell Beach, a part of me knowing that I would move here when the boys no longer needed me so much. The morning sun was low and there was a haze in the air, adding a dreamy edge to the vista. Shards of pure light bounced off the waves as they crashed and sizzled up the sand beside me.

In the distance, I could see a lone walker, and a black dog racing in and out of the sea with tail wagging. A simple scene, but so joyous. As they neared, my heart sped up. Was it? No, I must be imagining what I wished to see. But wait...

The figure stopped. The dog dropped a red ball at his feet, looking up at him expectantly. Then the man ran across the sand, faster, sprinting towards me. When he swept me into his arms, tears were already streaking my cheeks.

'Belle, my love. I hoped I'd find you here.'

I had no words. He bent down and kissed me so tenderly, then passionately.

The wet dog pushed against us, and we separated, giggling.

'Belle, meet Tobes,' he said.

'Hi Tobes,' I said, patting the dog's head.

Isaac pulled me to him, cupped my face in his hands and looked deep into my eyes.

'Take that chance, Belle. Marry me.'

'Yes,' I said, 'I will.'

Dear Sheba,

The last year has been a whirl, so I am sorry not to have written. I know you'll be happy to hear it's been a perfect year. Isaac is the one. The boys love him, and I love his girls. When we all meet up, it makes my heart shine to see so many smiling faces around the table. We have seen each other more and more, and a few months ago, Sheba, you won't believe this, we attended the Royal Garden Party together. Well, not together, I went with our former Civic Mayor and Isaac was with the Mauritian ambassador. What are the chances! We both looked the part in our smart outfits and the queen was stunning in a daffodil yellow outfit. It felt like the most natural thing in the world to be somewhere like that with him. I feel I can go anywhere with his support. There are no limits. And here's the real news, Sheba… tomorrow, we marry in Cornwall! In fact, on Holywell beach where we shared our first kiss. Family and friends have filled hotels, B&Bs and cottages for miles around. After our honeymoon in Bali, we are moving into his cottage here with the girls and Toby the dog. There's room for the boys to come and stay in the holidays and they are keen to go surfing. I am so blessed, Dearest Sheba, and I thank you for all the years you have listened to my heart. Forgive me if I am absent from now on but know that it is only because I am finally happy. I am finally the Belle we dreamed of me becoming.

Your Belle xx

My Dear Reader,

Here is where we must exit the roller coaster of Belle's life. I wish for her only the tiniest of dips and long steady climbs from now on. She deserves her sunshine and smiles. As do we all. Take heart if you are low and appreciate your highs for all of us must travel the ups and downs of life. And all of us should find our own path to convert our pain into purpose and do good with it. We should all be a little bit Belle...

Sheba x

ACKNOWLEDGMENTS

Thank you to my two brothers and parents who have been a great and reliable support throughout my life.

Thanks to Jason for designing such a creative book to make it feel like a unique diary.

I want to thank all those people I have crossed paths with either at work, the council, all the brave Nurses & Doctors who shared their story and to my amazing family and friends.

I hope the diary will inspire those who are struggling in life to start writing in a diary to express your thoughts and feelings.

Life is like a cake we have to make very slice taste better than the last and always strive to be the best version of yourself.

My dear reader you can do this....